characters created by

# lauren child

# We honestly CAN look after your dog

PUFFIN

**Charlie and Lola** ™

Text based on script written by Bridget Hurst and Carol Noble

Illustrations from

the TV animation

produced by Tiger Aspect

PUFFIN BOOKS
Published by the Penguin Group: London, New York, Australia,
Canada, India, Ireland, New Zealand and South Africa
Penguin Books Ltd, Registered Offices: 80 Strand, London WC2R 0RL, England

puffinbooks.com

First published 2005
Published in this edition 2007, reissued 2008
1 3 5 7 9 10 8 6 4 2
Text and illustrations copyright © Lauren Child/Tiger Aspect Productions Limited, 2005
The Charlie and Lola logo is a trademark of Lauren Child. All rights reserved
The moral right of the author/illustrator has been asserted
Made and printed in China
ISBN: 978-0-141-50104-8

Original recording © Tiger Aspect Productions Limited, 2006
Copyright in this recording ℗ Penguin Books, 2007. All rights reserved
This edition manufactured and distributed by Penguin Books Ltd 2007, reissued 2008

I have this little sister Lola.
She is small and very funny.
At the moment Lola really, really wants to have a dog.
But Mum and Dad say she can't because our flat
is too small and Lola is too young to look after one.

Lola says,
"Say woof, Charlie."

So I say,
"Woof."

Then Lola says, "Sit!"

So I sit.

My
cereal
bowl

is

now

a dog bowl.

And she has made me a **dog** bed.

Lola just loves **dogs**.

A lot.

One day Dad took us to the park.

There was me and my friend Marv,
Lola and her friend Lotta.
And Sizzles.

Sizzles is Marv's dog.

## Lola loves Sizzles.

So does Lola's best friend, Lotta.

Lola says, "You ask."
Lotta says, "No you ask."

So Lola says,
"Marv, can we look after Sizzles?"

Marv says,
    "Lola, do you know
about dogs?"

Lola says,
"Yes I do. Everything."

And Lotta says, "So do I."

Lola says,

"We know that Sizzles is a very extremely very clever dog.
We know he can do very good tricks."

Lotta says, "If he wanted he could roll over."

Lola says,
"And **dance**.
**Definitely**, I think.
Lotta, do you know
I think
Sizzles
**can do**
**really**
**anything."**

Lola says,
"And
**walk**
on
**two**
**legs."**

Lotta says,
"And **speak English."**

Then Lola says, "Sizzles is the cleverest dog ever, anywhere."

Marv says, "Yeah. Watch this. Sizzles. Sit, Sizzles! Sit!

Sit!

Sit, Sizzles?"

While Marv is trying to
make Sizzles sit, I see some of our
friends playing football
and I think I'd really like to play too.

So I say,
"We could play just one game,
Marv?"

Marv says,
"But who is going to look after
Sizzles?"

Lola says, "**Me!**"

Lotta says, "**Me!**"

I say,
"It is only for a little while.
He'll be OK with Lola and Lotta.
I'm pretty sure he will."

So Marv says,
       "OK.
    But you do know that
there are lots of **rules**
       if you want to
              **look after** Sizzles.

No **chocolates.**

Or **cakes.**

And
       no **sweets**
of **any** kind.

Completely
no digging...

and

no chasing birds.

And

no s p l a s h i n g
in
puddles.

And
NO
taking him
off the
lead."

Marv says,
    "Do you honestly promise to
look after my dog?"

            Lola says, "Honestly,
        we do promise honestly,
                to look after your dog."

    Lotta says,
        "Honestly and promisedly, we do."

Lola says,
"Dogs must be stroked and patted."

Lotta says,
"To tell them we're their friend."

Lola says,
"Playing... is
    what makes dogs happy."

Lotta says,
"And grooming makes dogs feel pretty."

Lola says,
    "Dogs must go outside
and must walk."

Lotta says,
    "Otherwise what is the point
of their legs?"

Then Lola says,
"Lotta, I don't think you really know
all about dogs like me."

And Lotta says,
"Lola, I really do know
everything about dogs."

Lola says, "But Lotta, I'm in charge."

And Lotta says,
"So am I."

Lola says,

"We're both in charge, but I think that I was a little bit more in charge than you. that Mary said

"You see, Lotta, you must hold the lead like this. See?" Lotta says, "Oh no, Lola. You really must do it like this."

# "Oh no!"

"Sizzles, where are you?"

"Where are you, Sizzles?"

"Sizzles,
where
are
you?"

Lola says,
    "Do you think we have
lost him **forever**?"

        Lotta says,
    "I think he was **sad** actually."

                Then Lola says...

**"Sizzles!"**

But then Lola says,
"Oh no! There are two Sizzleses!"

And Lotta says,
"No, Lola, there are two dogs.
But only one is Sizzles."

Lola says,
"But which one?"

Lotta says,
"I don't know."

Lola says,
"The clever one!
Sizzles can do anything, remember?"

Lotta says, "Yes. **Sizzles** can do **anything...**

... **Sizzles** can sit!

Sizzles! Sit. Sit. Sit!"

And Lola says,
"Sit. Sit. Please sit!"

Lotta says,
"Sit, sit, sit.
Will you sit!"

Then Lola says,
"Sizzles! It's Sizzles!"

When me and Marv finished playing football,
we went to find Lola and Lotta.
I say, "Come on, you two. It's time to go."

But Lola and Lotta look a bit fidgety.

And they both whisper,
"Charlie, we had Sizzles
and we were
looking after him..."

then he sort of went for a walk...

without his lead.
And then we couldn't see him any more.
And then we saw him but he wasn't one,
he was two Sizzleses.

And so... I'm not sure

that Sizzles
is
Sizzles now."

So I say, "Look here! Dog number: 144. Sizzles.
Owner: Marv Lowe,
5a Crocodile Street."

Then Marv says,
"That's his dog tag. It's got his name and address on it,
in case he gets lost.

All dogs have them."

And Lola says,
　　"We knew that **actually**, Marv."

And Lotta says,
　　"Just in case
they get **lost**."

I say,
"Yes, **that's right**.
　　Just in case
they get
　　lost!"

And Lola says, "But Sizzles would never get lost."
Lotta says, "Because he's very clever."
Lola says, "He can do absolutely anything."
And Marv says, "Come on, Sizzles, we're going home."